Family Magic #2

Hexed
Hair

Enjoy!! :)

jenlott

"You'll never brush your hair again!"

by Jennifer Lott
illustrated by Doriano Strologo

Hexed Hair
Book #2 of the Family Magic Series

Copyright © 2014 by Jennifer Lott

Reality Skimming Press
An Imprint of Okal Rel Universe
201-9329 University Crescent, Burnaby, BC, V5A 4Y4, Canada

Interior design: Lynda Williams
Cover & interior art: Doriano Strologo
ISBN: 978-0-9921402-5-0

Library and Archives Canada Cataloguing in Publication

Lott, Jennifer, 1987-., author
    Hexed Hair / Jennifer Lott, author; Doriano Strologo, Illustrator.

(Family magic ; 2)
ISBN 978-0-9921402-5-0 (pbk.)

    I. Strologo, Doriano, 1964-, illustrator II. Title.

PS8623.O87C87 2014   JC813'.6   C2014-900842-2

First Edition
(C-20140830)

Dedication

by Jaedyn, age 8

Visit familymagicseries.com to enter the next drawing contest for the dedication page.

Chapter 1

Charlotte loved the weekend, because it meant she could blow things up on the computer without an early bedtime interrupting. Saturday night at 9:00 p.m. that was exactly what she was doing.

Her big sister, Glenda, was reading a book on the couch. Her little sister, Eileen, stood astride the stick of a toy horse with the reins in her hands.

"Clear the runway!" Eileen cried as she prepared for her forty-seventh gallop down the hall.

"All clear," asserted Glenda from behind her book.

"Neigh!" whinnied Eileen. She tore across the room.

Their mother came upstairs, saw Charlotte on the computer, and stopped. "Charlotte, have you washed your hair yet?"

Since blowing up the wrong thing would kill her, Charlotte decided not to risk a distraction by answering.

"You haven't!" said her mother,

coming closer. "It's been three weeks now and you said you would wash it tonight."

"Yes!" cried Charlotte in triumph, as the screen announced her completion of the level.

"Yes," her mother agreed, "so you'd better go do that now."

"Eileen hasn't washed her hair," said Charlotte.

"Why don't you set her a good example and go first," suggested Glenda, peering over her book.

"That's not fair!" said Charlotte. "Why can't Eileen set me a good example, for once?"

"This is ridiculous!" her mother stormed. "Your hair needs washing!

It's something that you have to do, just like brushing your teeth or, or…"

"Blowing things up on the computer," said Glenda.

Charlotte's eyes bulged in shock. "It's that important?"

"How can you even stand it?" her mother ranted on. "Your hair is a rat's nest! I bet you haven't even brushed it!"

"I have so!" said Charlotte, offended. "I brushed it ten days ago!"

Glenda laughed. "If I didn't brush my hair for that long I'd have to cut it off; I'd never be able to untangle it."

"That's because your hair's so long," said Charlotte, matter-offactly. "When your hair is as short as mine, you only need to brush it once a month and wash it twice a year."

"Charlotte!" said her mother. "What will people think of me if I send you and Eileen to school on Monday looking like ragamuffins? Poor kids, they'll think, their mother can't even keep their hair clean!"

"Neigh!" whinnied Eileen, now on her fifty-eighth gallop, and completely oblivious to the conversation.

"If you can't take care of your hair," said their mother, "then you should just…"

"Shave it off," said Glenda, smirking.

Charlotte made a face at her. "You're so weird."

Their mother moved between them. "Do you have a better idea, Charlotte?"

"We'll wash our hair first thing in the morning," said Charlotte, turning back to the computer.

"And you, Eileen?" her mother asked, looking around for her.

"Neigh!" Eileen pulled up on her reins and stopped running. "What, mommy?"

"Will you wash your hair first thing in the morning?"

"Yes, mommy," said Eileen.

Their mother took a deep breath and let it out slowly. "I'll believe it when I see it," she said.

Chapter 2

When Charlotte got up the next morning, Eileen was already scraping toast crusts into the kitchen garbage. Their mother was standing at the counter, drinking coffee. Charlotte went to put her own bread in the toaster.

"You still haven't washed your hair, either of you," her mother said, looking from one to the other.

"Can't we wash it tomorrow?" said Eileen.

"That's what you said yesterday," her mother accused.

"How about we brush our hair

today and we wash it tomorrow," Charlotte suggested.

"Arrrh!" said her mother.

But at that moment, her father came into the kitchen with Glenda. He had a dirty cereal bowl in his hands.

"You forgot to wash my favourite bowl," he was saying to Glenda. "I found it in my bed this morning."

Eileen giggled. "You forgot something too, daddy!"

He looked surprised. "No, I didn't."

"Yes, you did," said Charlotte.

He shook his head and started to give the bowl to Glenda, "You better wash this now. I can't have my breakfast without—" But the bowl disappeared before it could reach her.

"Oh, daddy!" said Eileen, as her father gaped at his empty fingers. "You'll never get your breakfast if you do it that way."

"But where? How? What?" he sputtered.

"Don't worry," said Eileen, encouragingly. "It's probably still in your room. If you hurry and find it, you can unspell it before it moves again!"

"Go on," her mother said to him. "I'll explain later."

Charlotte watched her father walk out of the kitchen. Then she looked at her mother with narrowed eyes.

"Mommy knows that Glenda's a witch," she whispered to Eileen.

"That's because you told her," said Eileen.

"I think she's known longer than that," said Charlotte.

The two orange cats distracted Eileen by rubbing themselves up against her legs. "Aww, Honey!" she cooed. "Rosey!"

Charlotte decided to finish breakfast. She sat beside Glenda at the table.

Meanwhile, Eileen took the cats into the living room. She pressed the demo button on the electric piano, tapping her fingers over the keys while the tune played by itself.

"Dance, kitties!"

She started twirling to the chime sounds, but her mother caught her shoulders and held her still.

"Cat show later," her mother said firmly. "Hairbrush now. You have to at least brush."

"Eileen, come play Candyland with me," Charlotte called from the hall.

"Okay," said Eileen, ducking out of her mother's clutches.

"You two come back here," their mother snapped.

"We will brush our hair," Charlotte promised. "Just not right now."

"I want you to do it now," she said.

"But, mommy," said Eileen, "you always say you want us to be in-de-pen-dent," she stretched the word out impressively.

"Yeah," said Charlotte, putting her hands on her hips. "And that means we decide when we do things."

Eileen nodded.

Their mother's mouth was very tight. She took both hairbrushes out of the bathroom and walked away with them.

"Why are you taking our brushes, mommy?" said Eileen. "We'll need them later."

"No, you won't," she said sharply. "You don't have to brush your hair ever again." She went downstairs.

"Whoo-hoo!" Charlotte punched her fist into the air. "We won!"

"She still sounded mad," Eileen said uncertainly.

"That's because we won," said Charlotte.

Glenda laughed. "Are you sure you don't want to brush your hair ever again?"

"Don't answer that," said Charlotte, pulling Eileen along to the board game closet.

"Charlotte," she said nervously,

"do you think Glenda will make our hairbrushes follow us around?"

"No," said Charlotte. She thought about it more and said in a stronger voice, "No way. She won't do anything to the hairbrushes now that mommy has them."

Chapter 3

"Good morning! Goo-ood morning! Time to get uh-up now!" Her father's usual wake-up song lifted Charlotte's eyelids.

She groaned; it was Monday morning.

"Up, up, up, up, up," her father insisted. "Breakfast is on the table."

His footsteps tapped loudly: he was wearing the wooden sandals he liked because of his flat feet. She heard him tapping away down the hall. Good. Now she could get comfortable again.

Her head was cold. She pulled

her blanket completely over it.

Her door creaked. "Charlotte?" said a timid voice.

"Eileen?" Charlotte peeked out; then snuggled under the blanket again. "Get out of my room."

"My head feels funny," Eileen

said worriedly. "I think it's going to float away like a balloon."

"You just had a bad dream," yawned Charlotte.

"Please check," her little sister pleaded. "You're good at finding out about magic spells."

"If your head turned into a balloon, you wouldn't be able to talk," said Charlotte.

"Are you sure?" said Eileen. "Did you read that in Glenda's spell book?"

"Go away," said Charlotte.

"Why are you under your blanket?" asked Eileen.

"My head is cold."

"Mine too," said Eileen.

"Balloons are cold, aren't they?"

Charlotte rolled over with another groan. "Your head is normal. Go back to bed."

"You didn't even look," Eileen protested.

"I'm not listening either." Charlotte threw the blanket off her face to show that she had her hands over her ears.

She was very glad that her ears were covered, because Eileen screamed.

"Hey!" Charlotte plugged her ears up better with the corners of her pillow. "Don't make daddy come early. He still thinks we're getting dressed."

Eileen tried to tug Charlotte's pillow away from her ears.

"Stop it!" Charlotte reached up to pull Eileen's hair.

She couldn't find it.

She grabbed Eileen's ears instead and pulled her whole head towards her. Their foreheads bonked together.

"Owww!" They sprang apart and looked at each other.

Charlotte sat up with a gasp.

"I-it's okay, Charlotte," said Eileen, patting her arm. "We can figure out how to fix you."

"Fix me?" Charlotte goggled at her little sister.

Above Eileen's eyebrows there was no hair. There was only shiny, bald skin.

"Feel your head!" Charlotte said urgently.

Eileen put her fingers on her scalp. Her lip quivered. "Wh-where did my hair go?"

"You better go look for it," said Charlotte. "Maybe your bed is cursed. Check under your pillow."

"What about your hair?" Eileen lifted Charlotte's pillow to check under it.

"What are you doing?" said Charlotte. "My hair is on my head."

"No, it's not," said Eileen.

"Yes, it…" Slowly, Charlotte raised her hands and felt all over her own head…her own smooth, hairless head.

She screamed louder than Eileen had.

"Shhh," said Eileen, "daddy's coming!"

Chapter 4

They could hear their father's sandals tapping louder. "What's going on? Charlotte, are you getting up?"

"No!" squeaked Charlotte. "I'm never getting up!"

They heard the sandals come even closer: tap, tap, TAP!

"You can't come in!" Eileen threw her back at the door and slid down to sit against it. "Ow!" she added as she bumped her bald head on the door.

"Eileen, why are you in there?" her father demanded. "You need to go get dressed."

The doorknob turned.

"Her clothes are in here!" Charlotte jumped out of bed and threw herself down to help block the door. She bumped her head too. "Ow!"

"Are you two okay?" He knocked loudly. "Charlotte, open this door."

"Maybe we should tell him," whispered Eileen.

"No," Charlotte hissed back. "He'll think we cut our hair off and get really mad. Or he'll put hats on us and make us go to school anyway."

"Oh no!" Eileen cried.

"What's the matter?" their father's voice said through the door.

"We're okay!" they said together.

"Well, hurry up, then," he said. "Mommy's taking you to school today, and she can't be late for work."

"We can't go to school today," said Charlotte.

"Why not?" he asked.

"We're sick," said Eileen.

"You just said you were okay," he said suspiciously.

"We're actually sick a-and itchy," Eileen babbled. "We both have big purple spots with—"

"You can stop there," said Charlotte.

"I don't know much about purple spot diseases," said her father, "but if you have a temperature—"

"We do!" Eileen assured him.

"We have a lot of temperature!"

"And," said Charlotte loudly, "it's contagious. So you can't come in and check."

"I was getting to that," huffed Eileen.

"Look—" their father was building up to his important voice now, "if you think you're going to get away with this—"

"Dad!" Glenda's voice called. "Hurry up! We're going to be late."

Charlotte breathed a sigh of relief. The words 'going to be late' were almost always enough to distract her father from anything else going on.

"I have to take Glenda to the airport," he said. "Go get mommy at 8:30; don't let her forget."

Seconds later, they heard the front door close: Glenda and their father were gone.

"That was close!" Charlotte

pushed herself up off her bedroom floor. "Come on, Eileen. We only have an hour to break the spell. We've got to get Glenda's spell book."

Eileen stood up too. She felt shorter without her hair. She only came up to Charlotte's shoulder, and she was sure it had been the chin before.

"Why is Glenda going to the airport?" Eileen asked.

"She's going to some festival in Disneyland to play with her band," said Charlotte. "Did you hear what I said about Glenda's spell book?"

"But we don't need the book this time," said Eileen. "Now we know how Glenda's spells work, we can break them ourselves."

"How?"

"By washing and brushing our hair!" beamed Eileen. "Because that's what—"

"We don't have any hair to wash and brush," Charlotte reminded her.

"Oh," said Eileen. Then she brightened. "We can use the spell book to grow our hair back and then we can wash our hair and break the spell!"

"Ahh…right," said Charlotte. "Good idea. Let's go do that."

Chapter 5

Wasting no time, they went straight to Glenda's computer. Charlotte took the driver's seat and double-clicked on the file labelled *Domestic Witchcraft for Teens*.

"You know," said Eileen thoughtfully, "the title makes it sound like there are other books for different ages. Do you think there's a *Domestic Witchcraft for Eight-Year-Olds*?"

"Don't be ridiculous," said Charlotte. "You're too young to be a witch."

"How would you know?" sniffed Eileen.

Charlotte, who was now typing 'no hair spells' into search, ignored her.

"Glenda could have been a secret witch for years," Eileen went on. "Maybe she learned it at school when she was little."

"But she went to the same school as us," said Charlotte, "and we're learning math and spelling."

"Yes…" Eileen scratched her bald head thoughtfully. "That could be it. A secret spelling club that people go to…"

"I meant putting the right letters in words, silly," said Charlotte.

"But witches need to learn that too," said Eileen, "so they don't say spells wrong. I'm going to ask Ms. Tonild if learning French words will teach me magic."

Charlotte rolled her eyes. "And I'll ask Ms. Yancey if finishing the multiplication board will make the tiles fly up and clap."

"Well," said Eileen, "who do you think taught Glenda magic?"

"No one," said Charlotte. "She found these books and taught herself."

"Wow," said Eileen.

"There's nothing," said Charlotte, clicking out of search. "Stupid computer! What part of 'no hair spells' does it not understand?" She sat back to look at all Glenda's files instead.

"Try that one," said Eileen, pointing. "That looks like a spell book."

Charlotte opened the file and the screen was filled with the big flashy title: *Easy-Peasy Self-Restoration Magicworks*. Underneath it said: 'Never-ending answers to your never-ending problems! Non-stop help to service your urgent needs! Whether it be a spinning torso, a jogging nose, or a missing belly button, we guarantee a speedy recovery snapped into action by your very own fingers! It's everything that you would expect and more!'

"Excellent!" Charlotte enthused. "I bet this book will have—" she typed 'grow hair back spell' into search. "Yes, it does!" she said, gazing proudly at the screen which told her that six items had been found.

"Eyebrow hair, armpit hair, beard hair," Charlotte read, "nostril hair, moustache hair and…head hair!"

Chapter 6

"This is easy," said Eileen, peering eagerly at the head hair section. "It doesn't even have weird words in it. It just says, one: lick your right hand—" she did so and went on doing what she was saying as she read it "—and rub it over the area where you want your hair to grow. Two: lick your left hand. Three: snap the fingers of your right hand."

"It can't be that easy," said Charlotte as Eileen finished. "I mean that's just so—" but she stopped at the sight of the thick, glossy strands of brown hair that were now sprouting from Eileen's head.

Eileen put a hand to her head and dashed to the mirror while Charlotte hastily licked her right hand.

Eileen smiled happily as her scalp became covered in hair.

"Hey!" Charlotte cried, having completed the three steps. "It doesn't work on me!"

"That's funny," said Eileen, turning around. "Maybe I can—"

"I don't need—" Charlotte began to protest.

But Eileen rubbed her wet right hand over Charlotte's head, licked her left hand and snapped her fingers.

Almost instantly, Charlotte's hair began to grow. Her mouth fell open. If Eileen could do it…why did the spell like her spit better? It didn't make any sense!

In under a minute, Eileen's hair was down to her shoulders and still growing. Charlotte's hair was not far behind.

"Uh oh," said Charlotte. "You forgot to tell the spell how short I like my hair."

"Mine too," agreed Eileen. "It's growing down my back now!"

"Wait a minute!" cried Charlotte in sudden panic. "This is one of Glenda's books. What if all the hair spells are fixed to grow hair back as long as hers?"

"Don't worry about that," said Eileen, "my hair is longer than Glenda's already."

"And mine's as long as hers now!" wailed Charlotte. She pulled a handful of her hair in front of her face, terrified. The hair seemed to be growing faster every second.

Eileen tripped over hers, which was starting to crawl down the hallway.

Charlotte ran for the kitchen just as her growing hair hit the floor.

She grabbed a pair of scissors off the counter and grabbed some hair in her other hand. As she opened and closed the scissors, she saw bits of hair detach from the mass and flutter away. With her feeble weapon she continued to battle her hair, but the hair was definitely winning.

Chapter 7

Eileen had attempted to follow Charlotte but was now lying on the floor outside the bathroom, her legs bound in tangled hair. "Charlotte!" she yelled. "What are you doing in there?"

"Cutting my hair!" Charlotte yelled from the kitchen.

"Is it working?" asked Eileen. "Has it stopped growing?"

"No!" howled Charlotte, dropping the scissors in horror, "I think I just made it worse!" The scissors had become entangled in her hair and were now scraping across the floor at an alarming pace as the hair continued to grow.

Eileen snaked her way into the bathroom, unable to break her hairy leg-lock. She flung herself at a bottle of shampoo, shouting out: "I'm going to try to break the spell!"

"How are we supposed to do that?" shouted Charlotte. "Lick our feet?"

"Maybe," said Eileen. "But I think I should try this first." She dumped the bottle of shampoo onto her head.

"What did you do?" asked Charlotte.

"I…" began Eileen, "made it worse," she concluded after a moment.

The bottle was carried away in the growing hair's flow. When Eileen tried to get up, her elbow slipped on the patch of hair she'd poured shampoo on.

She wriggled back up the

hallway. She made it to a tall table by the front door. She grabbed onto the tablecloth that hung from the edge of this table to the floor. With her other hand, she grabbed as much of her hair as she could.

"What are you doing now?" Charlotte's voice called from the kitchen.

"I'm putting – my hair – under the – Going Away Table!" Eileen panted, as she stuffed handful after handful past the hanging cloth.

Charlotte was astonished. "Why?"

"Because I want it to go away!" Eileen shrieked.

"That table is just for things like

library books that are going away," Charlotte yelled back. "I'm licking my feet. Yuck! There's hair on my—"

A loud clattering and some muffled thumps drowned out the rest of her words.

Eileen stopped what she was doing. "Charlotte! Did something fall on you?"

"No," said Charlotte. "My hair's knocking pots off the shelves, then catching and tangling them."

"Maybe it wants our stuff," said Eileen, who by now thought the hair must have a mind of its own. "Maybe if we give it all our really good toys, it will let us go."

"No, Eileen! We can't give it

what it wants. It's just being a bully."

"But I'm scared of bullies,"
said Eileen, and sniffled. "I'm going
to open my closet, so it can get my

horse."

"No, not your horse!" cried Charlotte. "Just wait. Try to be brave. I'm coming!"

Chapter 8

Charlotte crawled across the kitchen, wading against the tide of hair. It was growing in a loop around her and out behind her, dragging pots and pans. It grew into her slippers and pushed them off her feet.

"Hey!" she yelled over her shoulder. "Give those back!" But the hair wound around her knees. She kicked until she was red in the face. "Get off! I have to save my sister, you evil—"

Then she noticed a mass of hair that was darker than her own. "Eileen," she said, grabbing the end of it, "is this yours?"

"Ow!" said Eileen, as Charlotte gave it a rough tug.

"I'll pull you over," said Charlotte, "just try and push with your arms and legs."

Bracing herself against the kitchen wall, Charlotte heaved at Eileen's hair. After a moment Eileen rounded the corner, lying flat on her back and covered in sheets of hair. "I wish I was bald again!" she whimpered.

Charlotte nodded fervently. "Me too," she said. "But if we can't stop this...hang on...I think the hair is growing down the stairs."

Eileen didn't need this put into words. At that very moment her hair got caught on the stair rail and she was dragged down the stairs, rolling and bumping along on her descending hair.

"Eileen!" cried Charlotte. "Come

back! We'll never break the spell if we just—"

But Charlotte lost interest in what she was going to say, as her hair tugged her down the stairs after Eileen.

"HELP! HELP! HELP!" Eileen screamed in muffled tones.

As Charlotte reached the bottom of the stairs, she caught a fleeting glimpse of Eileen under a pile of hair as big as a haystack.

Charlotte struggled towards Eileen and managed to dig one of her hands out of the mound.

"Come on!" yelled Charlotte over Eileen's continued screaming, "Hold my hand! I'll pull you out!"

"I WANT MOMMY!" screamed Eileen.

"Let's go to her office," said Charlotte. "She's probably writing."

Charlotte lost Eileen's hand as her hair grew to new heights.

Together they rolled across the floor, blinded by hair and powerless to resist its choice of direction.

Eileen was still screaming and Charlotte, now thoroughly panicked, joined in.

"MOMMY! MOMMY! HELP! HELP!"

Chapter 9

A hand came out of nowhere and clamped itself onto Eileen's scalp. Charlotte yelped in pain as a second hand dug fingernails into hers. In an instant, they both felt extremely light-headed. Brushing hair from her eyes, Charlotte saw that her hair had detached itself from her head. It lay all over the floor and had half of their mother's office tangled in it, but it had stopped growing.

Standing over them with uncharacteristic fury in her face, was their mother.

"Mommy!" gasped Eileen, climbing out of her hair. "Oh, mommy! Glenda put another spell on us and we tried to fix it, but it didn't work and our hair was eating us up and we were screaming and screaming, did you hear us, mommy?"

"You broke the spell!" Charlotte realized. "How did you—"

"How," interrupted their mother, "did you manage to turn

this house into a wig factory?"

"We—" Eileen began.

"Broken china! Clogged-up plumbing! Cats covered in—"

"Oh, no!" cried Eileen, who had quite forgotten their pets.

"We didn't mean to—" quailed Charlotte.

"Destroy my office!" demanded their mother.

"But Glenda's book told us to—"

"Glenda's book?" repeated their mother, more calmly. "Of course. Did it say that it would give you 'never-ending answers to your never-ending problems' and 'non-stop help to service your urgent needs'?"

"Yes," said Charlotte.

Their mother seemed to be fighting back a smile. "Was it 'everything that you would expect and more'?" she asked.

Eileen nodded.

"And you found that book on Glenda's computer, did you?" said their mother, looking angry again. "I thought Glenda got rid of it after she tried to use it to restore her lost belly button! You'd think that being covered in belly buttons would teach her something about manipulative advertising!"

"Glenda lost her belly button?" Charlotte marvelled.

"And now you've lost your hair," said their mother. "I hope that's taught you something."

"How can we fix it?" asked Eileen.

"You can pack this mess into garbage bags and take it to the dump."

"But what about…" Eileen gestured hopefully at her bald head.

"It'll grow back," said their mother, smugly. She left the room.

"That's so unfair!" Charlotte raged. "It's not our fault we lost our hair! It was Glenda and that stupid book!"

"I don't think it was Glenda," said Eileen.

Charlotte looked over at her. Eileen was staring at their mother's 'Mist of Dreams.' It was a decorative humidifier: an elegant glass bowl on a handsome metal stand. The bowl was full to the brim with water that was billowing off the surface in sheets of mist.

At the bottom of the bowl were their hairbrushes.

Chapter 10

Charlotte and Eileen struggled up the stairs, winding hair around their arms as they went. They found their mother sitting on a cleared patch of floor in front of the Going Away Table, reading a book. She didn't look up, and they didn't feel like talking just then.

Charlotte wasn't afraid of Glenda, but she was a little worried her mother might be scarier. Eileen felt that it would be better to talk again when daddy got home.

Soon enough, they heard the van crunch over gravel in the icy driveway. Big boots came up the stairs, being extra noisy as they stomped off snow.

Their mother looked up. She lifted the cloth covering the space under the Going Away Table and

wiggled backwards until she was sitting in that space. The cloth dropped, hiding her from view.

Since their mother had been known to take a book into a closet for a little peace and quiet, Charlotte and Eileen didn't find it that strange.

Their father stomped through the door. "Charlotte! Eileen!" His mouth was wide with late-for-school shock. "Didn't I tell you to get mommy out of her office at…" And then his mouth opened wider with bald-daughters-and-hair-all-over-the-house shock.

"We didn't think we should remind mommy when it was 8:30," Eileen explained. "She got upset about the hair mess we made."

"It was her fault!" Charlotte ran to hug her father. She swung her head up from his middle, staring him seriously in the face. "Remember the cereal bowl, daddy? How Glenda put a spell on it?"

"Mommy, tell daddy how you're a witch too," Eileen invited, lifting the cloth on the Going Away Table.

There was nobody there.

"She was under the table!" Eileen looked wildly back at her father. "Where did she go?"

"To work, I hope," he grumbled, glancing at his watch.

Charlotte was amazed that even he could care about time at a moment like this. "Daddy," she said, "don't

you think we should do something?"

"You're right." He started kicking a path through the hair. "I'll get some garbage bags."

"Not yet," said Eileen, digging with her hands. "Help me save the kitties!"

"But what do we do about mommy?" Charlotte said impatiently. "Have you seen her office, daddy? Her Mist of Dreams is really a cauldron!"

Eileen dragged a cat up by the paws and scooped its bum to her chest. "We could make wigs for our heads, Charlotte," she said, looking at the dirty-blonde hairs that hung off the cat's ears. She dropped that cat onto the hair-covered couch, and began hunting for orange elsewhere.

"Mommy used our hairbrushes to cast the spell!" said Charlotte.

"She made us bald, daddy," Eileen chimed in, "and we grew it back only we didn't mean to grow it so much."

"We're surrounded!" said Charlotte. "I think mommy started the whole thing."

"Poor kitty!" Eileen concluded, lifting the other one out of the mess.

There was silence while Eileen cuddled both cats on the couch, and Charlotte stood staring at their father.

A horrible thought was occurring to Charlotte. She'd thought she knew Glenda. She'd thought she knew her mother. But, no, not her father too…

"Daddy?" she said in a small voice.

He sank onto the couch with a big sigh. "Charlotte," he said, drawing her down beside him. "Eileen." He put his arm around her, and looked slowly from one to the other. "I knew when I married your mother that I'd be in for a few surprises."

Made in the USA
Charleston, SC
15 December 2014